Curious George®

Snowy Day

Adapted by Rotem Moscovich
Based on the TV series teleplay written by Lazar Saric

Houghton Mifflin Company Boston 2007

For information about permission to reproduce selections from this book, write to Permissions, Houghton Mifflin
Company, 215 Park Avenue South, New York, New York 10003.

Library of Congress Cataloging-in-Publication Data

Moscovich, Rotem.
Curious George snowy day / adaptation by Rotem Moscovich.
    p. cm.
    "Based on the TV series teleplay written by Lazar Saric."
    ISBN-13: 978-0-618-80043-8 (pbk. : alk. paper)
    ISBN-10: 0-618-80043-3 (pbk. : alk. paper)
    I. Saric, Lazar. II. Curious George (Television program.) III. Title.
    PZ7.M8494Cur 2007
    [Fic]—dc22
    2006101437

Design by Joyce White
www.houghtonmifflinbooks.com

Manufactured in Singapore
10 9 8 7 6 5 4 3 2 1

George woke up to a wonderful surprise. It had snowed all night!

George was curious about all that clean, white snow. Maybe he could build something out of it.

"You go outside, George," said the man with the yellow hat. "I'll make us some cocoa for later."

This was going to be a perfect day. George went out to play. Uh-oh! He sank right into the fluffy powder!

Bill, George's friend and neighbor, came by. He did not have any trouble walking on the snow. "Hey, George," Bill said. "I have an extra pair of cross-country skis you can have."

Then Bill showed George how to ski by making zigzags through the snow. George could not wait to try it for himself.

With skis George could stay on top of the snow, and he followed Bill uphill.
Suddenly, they heard a noise. OINK! OINK, OINK, OINK!

Bill said, "I'm going to go find out what that is. You wait here."

George waited on top of the hill in the cold. His house looked so small and warm. George wanted to get home for his cocoa. Was Bill coming back?

"Hey, George!" Bill shouted from the bottom of the hill. "I couldn't find whatever made that sound. But I have to head home now! Keep the skis and have fun!"

So George did . . . for a while.

When George was tired, he skied down the hill toward home—until he hit a rock! His skis flew off, and George tumbled the rest of the way down.

George picked himself up at the bottom of the hill. What would he do now?

He spotted two children pulling a sled. They were walking on the snow—but they did not have skis. How did they do it?

It had to be those wide flat shoes they wore.

"Vinny, I think he likes our snowshoes," the girl said.

George nodded.

"Vicky and I live on the other side of the hill," said Vinny. "If you come home with us, we'll lend you our snowshoes so you can get home too. Climb aboard the sled!"

It was fun to sail down another hill, but now George was even farther from his house.

"Here you go, monkey," Vicki said. She gave George her snowshoes and climbed on the sled. "Bye, monkey. Good luck!"

George began his long journey home. He was cold and tired, and climbing up the hill was hard work.

The thought of a nice steaming cup of cocoa kept him going.
OINK!
George looked up. There was that noise again. He decided to follow it.

A cold, lost pig!

What was he doing out here all by himself? And how could George rescue the poor pig?

George remembered how Vicki and Vinny had rescued him.

What George needed was a sled. It had to be flat and big enough for the pig to sit on. A fallen sign nearby looked like a good choice.

What a ride!

When George got home, he found his neighbor, Farmer Renkins, talking to the man with the yellow hat.

"Thanks for bringing my pig home, George!" the farmer said. "He got out last night before it snowed."

"Good work, George," said the man with the yellow hat. "There's some cocoa waiting for you inside."

That was exactly what George had hoped to hear.

Skiing, snowshoeing, sledding, and now cocoa . . . it had been the perfect snowy day.

SNOW SMART

George and his friends were able to travel through the deep, fluffy snow with the help of . . .

AUTOMOBILE **SNOWSHOES** **ROLLER SKATES** **SKIS** **MOTORBOAT**

BOOTS **BICYCLE** **SLED** **ROCKET** **WOODEN SIGN**

DO YOU KNOW WHY?

George sank into the snow when he was wearing snow boots because he was heavier than the snowflakes underneath him. But he stayed on top of the snow when he wore skis or snowshoes because the larger area of the skis and snowshoes spread George's weight over many more snowflakes.

HELP GEORGE GET HOME!

Which track should he follow to get down the hill?

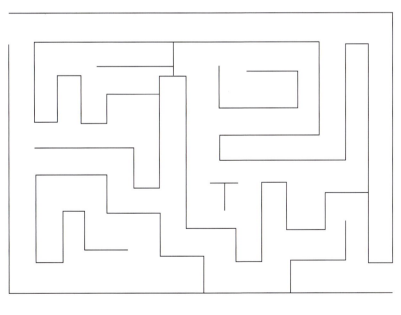

LET IT SNOW!
Make your own snowflake

Materials:
A few sheets of square paper
Safety scissors (or ask an adult for help)

INSTRUCTIONS:

1. Fold the top edge of the paper down to the bottom edge.
2. Fold the left edge over to the right edge.
3. Turn the square so that the corner with all the folds (no open edges!) is at the bottom. Fold the corner on the right side over to the left side, making a triangle.

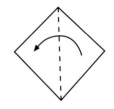

4. Cut off the tip opposite to the fold corner. It can be pointed or rounded—experiment and see how different designs look.
5. Cut out shapes from the edges. The more shapes you cut out, the better.

Open up your snowflake when you are finished cutting. You should have a lovely pattern. Now you can paste it on some colored paper, put it up in your window, or hang it on a tree!